The Adventures of THANDIE The Tandem

The Adventures of THANDIE The Tandem

Claire Le Block

First published 2018

Published under licence by Brown Dog Books and
The Self-Publishing Partnership, 7 Green Park Station,
Bath BA1 1JB

www.selfpublishingpartnership.co.uk

ISBN printed book: 978-1-78545-269-7

Illustrations by Tim Hole
Cover design by Andrew Prescott
Internal design by Andrew Easton

Printed and bound in the UK

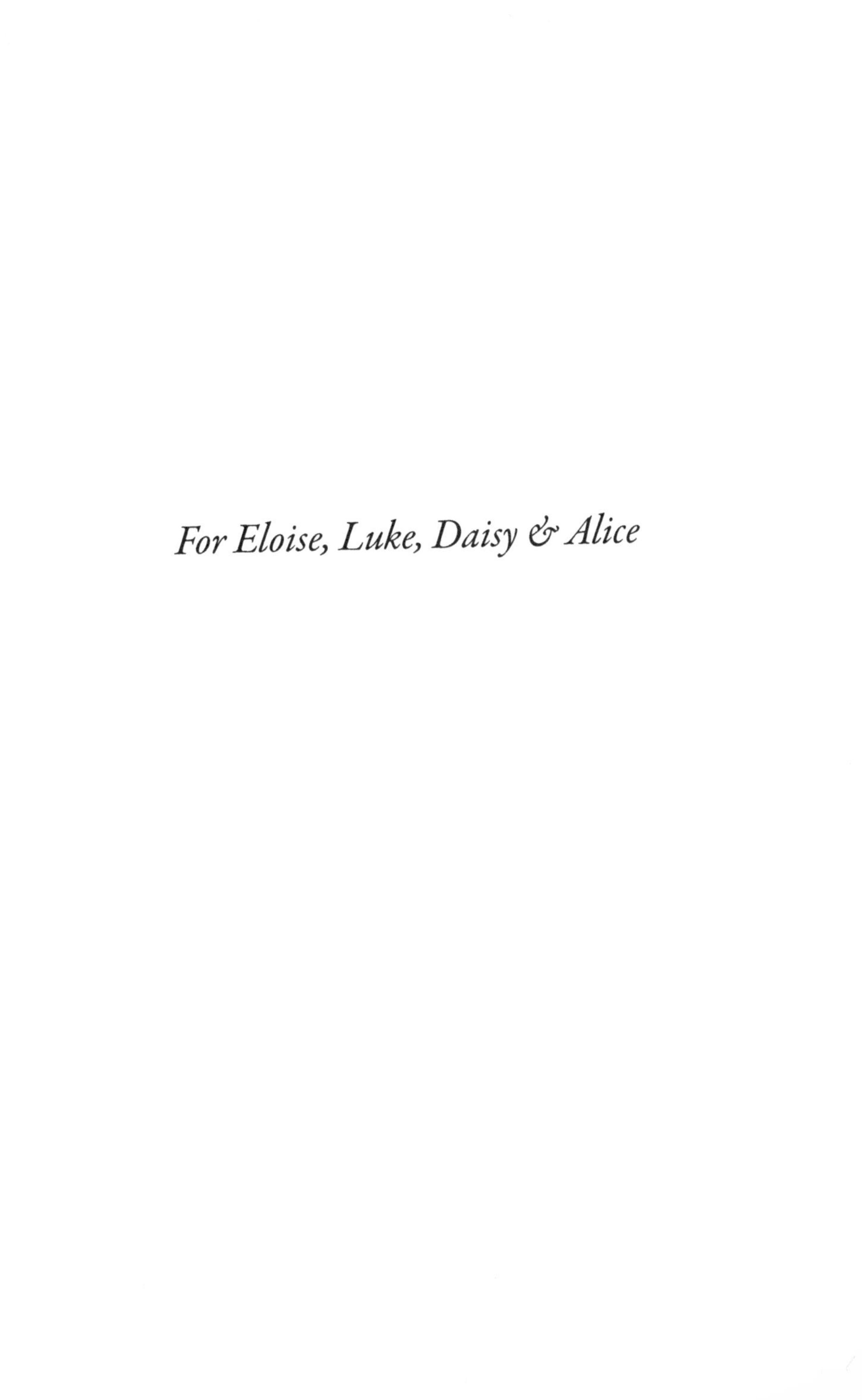

For Eloise, Luke, Daisy & Alice

Timmy and Thandie's adventures are based on real experiences. Thandie (pronounced Tandy) is short for Thandiwe which means 'Beloved' in several southern African languages. She is a real tandem bicycle that has cycled through more than 30 countries, in four continents, giving lifts to hundreds of people.

Timmy and Thandie's route

Uncle Max's letter

The letter had arrived nearly two weeks ago, a postcard from Uncle Max.

POST CARD

Dear Timmy,

Sorry, I havent written for a while
but things have been really busy.
The elephants are in danger. My old enemy, Mr
Kubwa, has become very powerful. I dont have
enough good people around me. Do you want
to come to live with me and help me protect
the elephants? I really need your help. The only
thing is that there is no way that I can come
to pick you up. I cannot leave the elephants
with Mr Kubwa around. My house is in Kenya, in
Africa. Thandie should be with you soon. She
will help you find me.

See you in a few weeks.
Uncle Max

Timmy did not know what to think. Uncle Max was his only living relative and he knew he would love to go to

Kenya to live with him and help him with the elephants. He didn't know why Uncle Max needed help or who Mr Kubwa was but he was sure he could find out and be helpful. He didn't understand about Thandie. Who was Thandie and how would she help him? But Thandie had not arrived and Timmy didn't think he could make it to Kenya on his own. The worst thing was that Timmy had boasted to his all his friends about going on an adventure to Africa to save the elephants from the evil Mr Kubwa. They all thought Timmy was making it all up.

It was now the first day of the summer holidays. Timmy and his best friend, George, were sitting on the wall outside the house where Timmy lived with Mrs Haddock. They were both bored. Timmy was kicking at a stone trying to see if it would fall out of the wall. George was teasing Timmy about Africa, elephants and some girl called Thandie. Timmy was trying to decide if going into the house to find Mrs Haddock and do his chores would be better than listening to George.

Mrs Haddock was Timmy's guardian and was always grumpy. She was thin and bony and had big, bulging eyes which magically saw everything he did. Her eyes made her look a bit like a fish and Timmy thought that was why she was called Mrs Haddock, although he never dared to ask her. He did all the jobs like washing up and taking out the rubbish.

Then, suddenly, there was a gigantic parcel, just sitting there at the front gate. Timmy pushed his messy brown hair out of his eyes and stared. George stopped going on about Africa and watched in amazement as the delivery man, huffing and puffing as he carried it to the doorstep, asked if there was an adult to sign for the package.

"Er… yes, Mrs Haddock's here."

Timmy rushed inside.

"Stop running," came a shriek from the huge armchair in front of the television. Timmy slowed down and pointed at the enormous parcel, bigger than Timmy himself, still standing by the front door.

"Hmmmph," mumbled Mrs Haddock, slowly and suspiciously rising to her feet and walking to the front door. "It seems to be for you," she said in surprise, handing Timmy an envelope. "Looks like nonsense to me," she said, turning back to the television.

Timmy recognised the writing, it was from Uncle Max.

Sorry Thandie's a bit late, we had a bit of trouble at passport control. It will all be fine now. She knows the way. See you soon.

A jumble of excited thoughts whipped through

Timmy's mind. He ripped the paper off the parcel and revealed a bicycle, but not a normal bicycle. It was really, really big, it was red and yellow and green, and it had two seats. Timmy thought it looked as if it had a face, just where the handlebars were. She seemed to be looking right at him and smiling.

"Are you Thandie?" he asked, feeling a bit silly, because who talks to a bicycle? It may have been his imagination but it looked as if Thandie's smile got bigger and she winked at him. "Do you know the way to Uncle Max in Kenya?" whispered Timmy. Again, Thandie seemed to wink back at him.

He heard another "Hmmmph" and turned to Mrs Haddock who had been reading the note over his shoulder.

"Uncle Max has finally sent me Thandie. Can I go to live with him now?" asked Timmy.

"Hmmmph," she mumbled again. "Max and his elephants. I didn't think we would hear from him again. It will be very hard to get there and very hard to live there."

It's pretty hard living here, he thought, glancing at the great piles of dirty dishes towering in the sink. "It sounds like an adventure. Thandie knows the way. Please can I go?" pleaded Timmy.

"Hmmmph, well, I suppose he is your only relative and

you might be useful to him and those silly elephants of his." She looked doubtfully at Thandie. "I'm not sure how a bicycle can know the way, even a big bicycle like this."

Timmy looked at Thandie and again she seemed to smile back at him. "Don't worry, I think we will be fine," he said happily. He turned excitedly to George, who was still staring at Thandie with a glum look on his face.

"So Thandie's a bike. She must be a magic bike. I guess you really are going to Africa," George said quietly.

Timmy realised that George was jealous. Timmy was going to have an amazing adventure, go to Africa with Thandie, meet his long-lost uncle, help the elephants, fight Mr Kubwa. George was going to spend the holidays in London, getting bored.

"Why don't you come with me for the first bit?" Timmy said, excitedly. "It looks like Thandie is meant to take two people." Thandie seemed to nod her handlebars and smile at the boys.

Timmy made a list and packed all his stuff into four bags, called panniers, which attached to either side of Thandie's wheels. He didn't need much as he knew it would be hot in Africa and he would just have to get a bit smelly. He thought happily about no one nagging him to have a bath or wash his clothes. He packed:

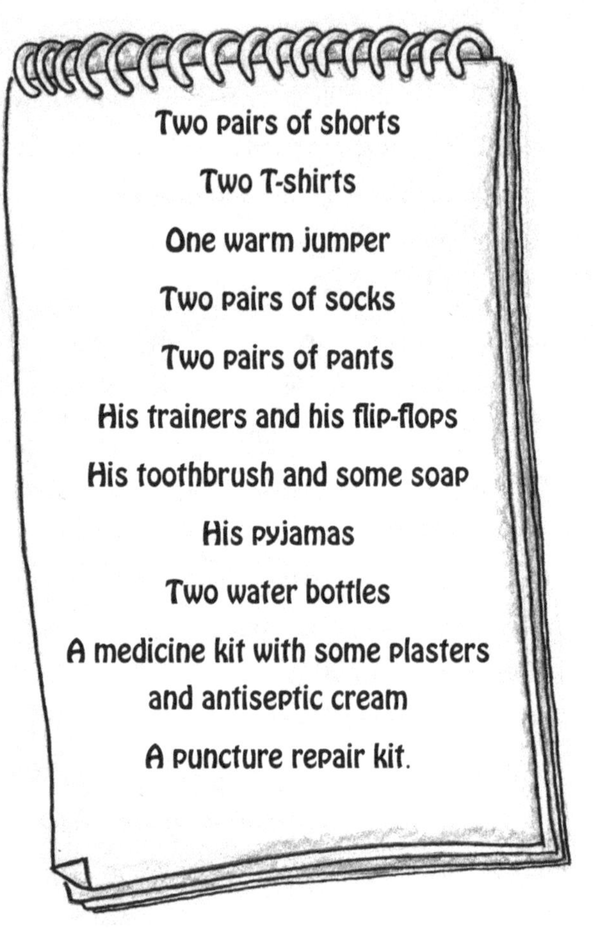

He went to bed more excited than he had ever been. The next morning, he woke up early and said goodbye to Mrs Haddock, who just gave a disgruntled "Hmmmph" and made some grumbling noises along the lines of "Who will do all the washing up now?" Timmy was too excited to pay any attention. George arrived and then they were ready to go.

The first bit was easy. They just had to get to Dover and then they could get a ferry to France. He put his panniers onto Thandie, who seemed to be smiling even more. "I bet you are very excited about our adventure too, Thandie," Timmy said. Thandie smiled and winked back at him.

A narrow escape

Timmy woke up to seagulls shrieking and the smell of salt in the air. He pushed his hair out of his eyes and rubbed them sleepily. He then remembered that he was on a ferry and Thandie the tandem bicycle was propped up next to him.

It is really happening, he thought. *I am on my way to meet Uncle Max in Africa.*

He had been having a lovely nap, recovering from the first couple of days of cycling. Cycling was really hard work! Waving goodbye to George in Dover seemed like years ago.

Timmy started to feel a little bit sad. He would miss George and his other friends. He wondered if he would make any more friends. Then he looked at Thandie, who looked as if she was smiling back at him. Timmy felt happier; Thandie was his friend.

Then he heard shouts but not in English. He realised that he was going to have to get used to different languages. Luckily, he knew a bit of French and so, as he pushed Thandie off the ferry, he asked one of the guards, "Où est Afrique?"

The guard looked at him in amazement, then pointed and said, "Au sud."

OK, Timmy thought. *I need to go south. Uncle Max and the elephants are in the south.* He felt very nervous. *What am I doing?* he thought, *I am just an ordinary boy. Why am I cycling to Africa?*

Thandie started moving forwards through the busy port. Timmy took a deep breath and started pedalling. He would have to trust Thandie.

In a few minutes they had made their way onto a quiet road and Timmy started to enjoy himself. He felt the wind in his hair and the sun on his face. He knew Thandie would not let him down. He knew that they could find their way to Kenya and help Uncle Max to save the elephants.

Lots of people waved and shouted at him.

"They must be so surprised to see a boy on a tandem. We must look very peculiar," he said to Thandie. Thandie was shaking her handlebars and trying to move across the road. "Stop it!" cried Timmy. He couldn't work out what was wrong with Thandie. They trundled along and Timmy started to daydream.

Suddenly, they juddered to a halt. Timmy was roughly

woken from his thoughts of elephants and Uncle Max. He looked down and saw that Thandie's front tyre was flat.

He pulled Thandie off the road just in time. There was a loud hooting and he saw a car whizz right past them. The car swerved past, still beeping its horn. He could hear the driver shouting angrily out of the window in French.

Timmy sat down by the side of the road feeling very shaken and upset. "Perhaps we are on a road that bicycles cannot use," he said sadly to Thandie.

Then a girl ran up to him, talking very quickly in French. Her big blue eyes looked worried.

"I'm sorry, I don't understand, I only know a little bit of French," said Timmy miserably. His first day in a new country was not going well.

"My name's Florence. Are you OK?" she asked kindly, in English. "I saw what happened, I was at the bus stop down the road. Why were you cycling on the wrong side of the road?"

"Of course! I am such a nincompoop!" Timmy cried. He looked at Thandie, who was looking very relieved. "You were trying to make us move to the other side, weren't you? I am so silly. I promise I will trust you next time." Thandie seemed to smile. Timmy turned back to Florence. "I forgot you drive on the wrong side of the road here."

"We don't drive on the wrong side, you do," she replied, smiling. They both laughed. "It's lucky you got that puncture and stopped," she said.

"Yes, very lucky," Timmy replied, thoughtfully. "Did you do that on purpose?" he whispered to Thandie. Thandie smiled sweetly back at him.

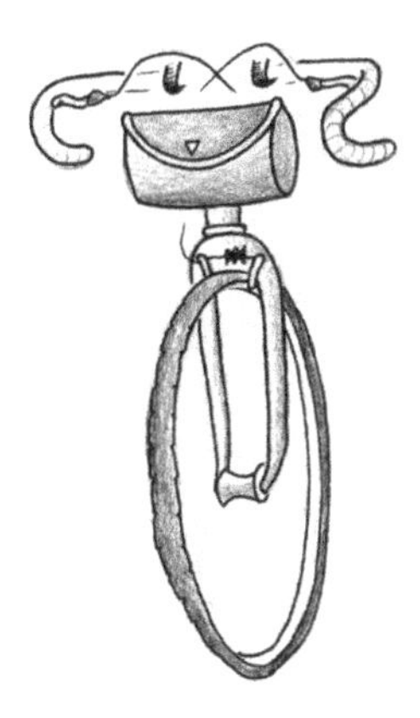

"I can help you mend the puncture," Florence continued. "I ride my bike all the time."

Timmy was very impressed that she knew what to do and, with both children working, the puncture was mended in no time. Timmy made sure he noted down how to mend it just in case he needed to do it again.

"Where are you going today?" Timmy asked.

"I'm waiting for the bus, I'm going to stay with my

aunt in Paris," she replied.

"That's south of here, isn't it?"

Florence nodded.

"We are going south, to Africa, to help my Uncle Max save the elephants. Jump on and we can give you a lift. I'm Timmy and this is Thandie."

"Thank you," she replied. "This is much more fun than the bus."

3

Timmy repays Thandie

Florence gave Timmy lots of advice about cycling in France and she told him which cities and landmarks to look out for to make sure he continued to travel south. He dropped her off by the Eiffel Tower and waved goodbye as she rushed off her aunt's house. Timmy looked up in awe at the huge tower, rising high above him.

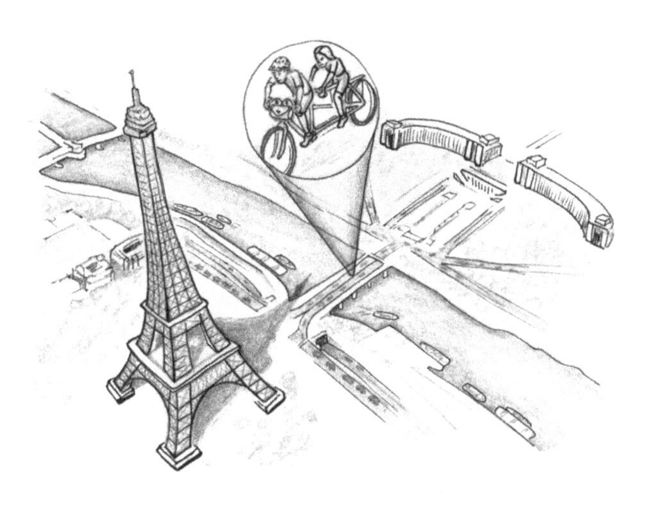

"Sorry, Thandie, I won't be long," he said as he locked

her to the railings.

Thandie looked at him sadly as he ran off and up the steps. He was very out of breath when he got to the top of the tower but the view from the top nearly took the little breath he had left in him away.

"Wow!" he breathed out heavily. "I bet I can see all the way to Africa from here!" He looked down below him, feeling a little bit sick, and saw Thandie. Even though Thandie was the biggest bike he had ever seen, she looked so small, far below him. He saw lots of people wandering about on the ground, all looking as small as ants busily moving around.

Suddenly, he saw a group of these ant-people heading towards Thandie. There was something about the way they were moving. He was certain that they were up to no good. They surrounded Thandie so that he could not see her any more.

"Hey, leave her alone," he shouted, but it was pointless. His words were taken away by the wind into the air and never reached the ears of the group on the ground. Timmy turned and fled out of the viewing deck. He ran down the stairs, taking them two at a time, as fast as he could. A few people shouted at him to stop, but he just knew he had to get to Thandie. He had a very bad feeling.

At last he was out on the ground and he ran, shouting and screaming at the top of his voice, towards the group of boys surrounding Thandie. He could see that they had a hammer and a saw – they were trying to break the lock and steal Thandie! Other tourists and people on their way to work stopped and stared at the strange boy with messy hair and clothes pushing past them, running as fast as his legs could carry him. The group around Thandie also turned to stare at him, then they stared at all the other people staring at them. They realised they were about to be caught red-handed and with a yell, they all ran off in different directions.

Timmy didn't care where they went, he just wanted to make sure Thandie was OK. He ran up and flung his arms around her. He thought she looked so scared and upset, as if she had been crying; droplets of water fell from her handlebars.

"I am so sorry, Thandie. I shouldn't have left you alone. We are a team. You are my best friend. Uncle Max and the elephants need us," he cried, his voice muffled as he continued to hug her. Thandie eventually seemed to smile, it was all going to be OK.

Slowly, they set off again. Florence had told Timmy that they should keep going south, over the Alps and cross into Italy. At the bottom of Italy, they could get a ferry to Alexandria in Egypt.

They met lots of very friendly people on their way and luckily, they did not have any more scary moments.

As they pedalled on, the temperature got hotter and hotter. Timmy got sweatier and sweatier (and probably smellier and smellier!). His messy hair was stuck to his face and he kept having to take off his helmet and pour cold water over his head. They went up and down, up and down through the mountains.

At last he made it across the border into Italy. He gleefully realised he could have pizza for lunch every day! He was doing so much exercise that he could eat whatever he wanted, but he still made sure he ate lots of fruit and drank lots of water too.

After a few more weeks, Timmy and Thandie made it to the port where they caught their second ferry. They settled down for a well-deserved rest on the ship's deck. They were getting used to cycling but it was still very hard work.

Timmy fell asleep dreaming of Africa, elephants and Uncle Max. When he and Thandie next cycled they would be in a new continent; they would be in Africa.

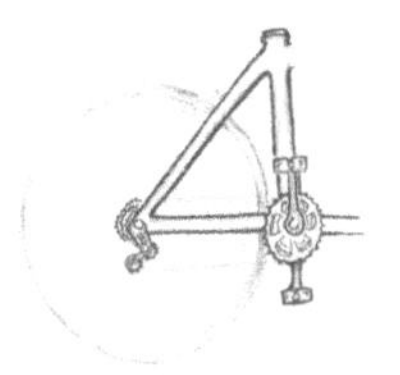

Cycling through the Pharaoh's' tombs

Timmy and Thandie had been in Africa for a couple of days. They were tired and hot and Timmy was probably a bit smelly as he had not had a shower since the ferry, but they were very happy. They were still cycling south, through Egypt, following the longest river in the world – The Nile. They were starting to get used to all the differences: the heat, the dust, the different smells, languages, clothes and customs. The people they met were always surprised to see them pedal past but they were always very friendly. Timmy was amazed at how many people had offered them food, water and somewhere to stay. He thought back to London and realised that people there were often quite unfriendly. He didn't think anyone in London would offer a strange, very smelly boy and his tandem bicycle somewhere to stay!

Soon they had made it to the pyramids. They stared up at the face of the sphinx.

"Isn't it strange?" murmured Timmy to Thandie. "The face of a man and the body of a lion. It might be the face of a pharaoh," said Timmy reading from a guidebook. "The Arabic name means 'Father of Dread' or 'Terrifying One'," he continued with a shiver.

They slowly made their way towards the biggest pyramid. Timmy craned his neck to look up to the top, nearly 140 metres above them.

"It's amazing that these are more than 4000 years old," Timmy said to Thandie as they pedalled slowly on. Then they heard a loud snort behind them. Thandie jumped; Timmy also jumped. They turned round and stared into the face of a camel. It was looking at Thandie in a very angry fashion. There came another snort and then a spitting noise and some disgusting stuff came out of the camel's mouth and landed on Timmy's head.

A voice came from the camel rider, "Sorry, she is being a bit naughty but I think she's scared of you. Only very occasionally does she spit on strangers. But she is confused. What sort of bicycle is that?"

Timmy was so angry and upset that he could not answer. He could feel Thandie shaking as the horrible, sticky mess trickled down the side of his face.

"Don't worry," said Timmy politely as they pedalled away from the camel as quickly as they could. "I have no idea why camels are so popular with tourists," he said to Thandie when they stopped so he could wipe it off properly.

She was still shaking. He looked down at her and realised that she seemed to be laughing! Timmy felt a spark of anger and then looked at Thandie's kind face. He felt the sticky mixture in his hair, and then he started to laugh too. He cleaned himself up and they set off again, south, towards the Valley of the Kings.

He had heard so much about these amazing structures, tombs for the ancient Egyptian Kings or Pharaohs. He knew that there were over 60 tombs and that dead bodies, called mummies, of royalty from thousands of years ago had been found there. He had heard about the curse of the pharaohs which brought bad luck, illness and even death to anyone who disturbed the tombs. He hoped it wasn't true!

They arrived at the famous site. It took Timmy's breath away; he and Thandie were utterly speechless. It was incredible. As they slowly wandered around they spent time trying to decipher the ancient Egyptian writing – hieroglyphics – which use pictures to represent sounds. Timmy worked out how to write his name and it looked really strange. He had to write *loaf of bread, reed, owl, owl, two reeds* to write TIMMY!

Timmy was very keen to find a real mummy, and so he went to find the legendary tomb of Tutankhamun. He left Thandie outside and crawled into every tomb, covering himself with dust and cobwebs. He was very happy, enjoying the experience of exploring, getting very dirty and dusty. Thandie was very happy having a rest in the shade.

They were having such a good time that they did not realise the sun was getting lower and lower. Timmy came out from a cave-like entrance and looked around. He pushed his hair off his face and tried his best to remove all the cobwebs. Luckily, stars were twinkling above them and when his eyes got used to the darkness he could see Thandie, looking a bit bored and fed up.

"Come on, Thandie, we had better go," he said.

They started pedalling towards where he thought they had come in, but they couldn't find the way out. The tombs were looming up, huge, above them. They were right in the centre of them. In the darkness they could hear sounds of animals scurrying about, enjoying the coolness of the night. They could also hear a strange banging and groaning coming from one particular tomb. Timmy shivered, his heart was beating so hard and so fast in his chest that he felt he might explode. Could the curse of the pharaohs be true? He knew he shouldn't have poked around so much in their tombs. Terrified, he and Thandie cycled on and on and on until he could bear it no longer; they were just going around in circles. They stopped and he sat down with his back to a large rock. He knew he had to last until morning and then it would all be better.

Just keep awake, Tim, he told himself, not wanting to fall asleep with all the terrifying and peculiar noises around them. He huddled closer to Thandie and tried to think of all his favourite things.

Then he heard a different noise, footsteps, soft and fast, as if someone or something small was running towards them. Timmy stiffened and felt his hair stand on end.

"Why are you still here and why are you talking to yourself?" came a voice through the darkness.

"I'm lost. Who are you?" replied Timmy in a very small voice. "I'm Nefertiti," came the answer.

Nefertiti, one of the great Egyptian queens! She has caught me red-handed in her tomb. What will she do me? These terrifying thoughts spun through Timmy's mind.

5
Guided by Nefertiti

"Queen Nefertiti, I am sorry I have disturbed you. Please forgive me. I got lost among your tombs and was waiting for morning."

He was very surprised to be answered with a giggle.

"Why are you calling me queen?" A girl of about his age appeared in front of him. She had huge brown eyes and her hair was hidden by a bright pink scarf. "I am staying with my uncle who is the manager here. You cannot stay out here all night. Come back to his house."

Timmy had never felt so relieved. He and Thandie followed Nefertiti out through the tombs.

The next morning, Timmy awoke to see Nefertiti and lots of other children playing on Thandie and trying to make her move. Thandie was not having any of it. Timmy ran over.

"Be careful, she's a very special bicycle," he shouted. "She is taking me south to Kenya, to my Uncle's house. We are going to help save the elephants."

"Why does she have two seats?" asked Nefertiti.

"So that we can give people a lift," Timmy replied, and Thandie seemed to smile.

"I need to go home to my family and they live in the south. Could you give me a lift?" she asked shyly.

Timmy looked at Thandie who smiled even more.

"Of course!" he replied. "You rescued us last night, so if you know the road south, then let's go."

Timmy and Thandie had made their first African friend.

"I can't believe you thought I was THE QUEEN Nefertiti!"

"I know, it was really silly," said Timmy, a little

embarrassed. "But I was thinking about all the ancient mummies and dead bodies and the Pharaoh's curse and it got dark…"

"I suppose the ancient Egyptians are very interesting to you," she said.

"Oh yes," Timmy agreed. "Much more interesting than any other history I know. Can you tell me more about your country?"

Timmy and Thandie settled happily into the rhythm of pedalling and listening as Nefertiti told her story. Timmy learnt all about ancient and modern Egyptians and the importance of the River Nile. He learnt about Nefertiti's religion and why she was wearing a headscarf, or hijab.

The silence was interrupted by the beautiful sound of the muezzin calling out the adhan. At first Timmy wondered what this noise was, this chanting he heard five times a day, starting at sunrise (it was a good alarm clock!). Nefertiti explained all about her religion, Islam, and that the muezzin was calling Muslims to prayer as they had to pray five times a day, facing East, facing Mecca, their sacred city.

The sound of the adhan meant they had arrived in Aswan, in the south of Egypt and Nefertiti's home. From Aswan, Timmy and Thandie did not have far to go before they crossed the border into Sudan, a country that is more than fifty per cent desert!

Beware of scorpions

Hot, hot, hot. Sand, sand, sand. That is all Timmy and Thandie could think about as they trundled along the desert road. At first it was unbelievably beautiful but now it just all looked the same – sandy. Now it just all felt the same – hot. It was so hot that Timmy and Thandie saw steam coming off the road. At first, they were shocked, as they thought something must be on fire but then the steaming, smoking roads became normal.

Timmy and Thandie were starting to get worried. Worried about water. They had entered the desert loaded with so many water containers that Timmy was not sure he and Thandie would have the strength to carry it all, but he knew they had to. Now they were running low and it was days since they had seen the river or a village. Timmy took another sip from his bottle; it was only a small sip but he finished it all. He looked at the other water bottles and twisted the lid off them one by one and tipped the last few drops into his parched mouth.

Timmy and Thandie needed a rest. Timmy needed to think about how he could get more water. At the next shady spot, sheltering under a huge sand dune, Timmy and Thandie stopped. Timmy took off his shoes to let his feet cool down (they were very sweaty and smelly, so it was a good thing only Thandie was around!). Then he put one of his panniers under his head. It was not long before they were both asleep, exhausted by the endless cycling, endless heat and worrying about water.

Timmy was woken up by a hard smack on his legs followed by a laugh.

"It nearly got you," came a voice.

Timmy rubbed his eyes and sat up slowly. He saw a smiling girl and then he nearly jumped out of his skin. In fact, he really did jump up and run behind Thandie when he saw a huge, red scorpion scurrying away.

The girl pointed at the scorpion and repeated, "It nearly got you."

"Thank you," stammered Timmy as he reached for his shoes.

"Stop!" shouted the girl. Timmy dropped his shoe and a smaller, red scorpion scuttled out. Then the girl prodded the other shoe with a stick.

"Just to make sure," she said. "They decided your shoes looked like a nice place for a nap."

Timmy plonked himself back down next to Thandie.

"Thank you," he said again.

"You shouldn't be out here on your own," said the girl. "Come with me to my village." She looked at the empty water containers. "We can give you some more water in return for you telling us all about who you are and your magical bicycle." She was staring in amazement at Thandie. "I'm Fadela, by the way."

More water and some company! Timmy and Thandie did not need to be asked twice. They got up and got ready to go.

"Hi Fadela, I'm Timmy and this is Thandie. Jump on!" With renewed energy the three of them set off again down the desert road.

"Welcome," said Fadela as they came to a cluster of huts. Goats and camels wandered around but not many people. "My family are all goat herders. I was out looking for some of our lost goats when I found you. We don't have much but we would like to invite you to be our guest."

Timmy had never felt so happy to see water, shelter and people, and never been so welcomed. They stayed with Fadela and her family until he got his energy back. He told them about London and Thandie and their adventures so far. He realised that at first, they found some things about him very strange just like he found some things about them very strange. But then he realised that they were not very different at all! He told them about Uncle Max and Kenya and how the elephants were in great danger. He asked if they could help him get to Kenya.

"Keep following the River Nile. Ethiopia is not far from here and after Ethiopia you will find Kenya," said Fadela, as he and Thandie got ready to leave.

Timmy said goodbye and thank you many, many times to Fadela and then he and Thandie set off again.

Ethiopia was very different from Sudan; it was more like being back in the Alps as they went up hills and down hills. They were exhausted but tried to look on the bright side.

"At least it's a bit cooler when we are up in the hills," said Timmy to Thandie.

Then they saw the border post for Kenya. Relief washed over Timmy in a great wave.

"Kenya, that's where Uncle Max lives. We are nearly there!"

7

Mungwe the Masai

Timmy woke up with the biggest yawn possible, so big he almost felt as if his jaw had been dislocated! The days were much cooler than in the desert but still much hotter than England and the temperatures that Timmy was used to. They tried to set off before dawn to cycle as much as possible when it was cool.

"Come on, Thandie, we had better get going," said Timmy, trying to sound more upbeat than he felt. "We've been in Kenya for days; it can't be far to Uncle Max's house." With a groan they set off, pedalling down the track.

Timmy shouted out in amazement as he saw a tall boy walking slowly down the road. He marvelled at the boy's purple cloak and stared with equal measures of fear and jealousy at the boy's sword and spear.

"Hello," said Timmy, "Who are you? What are you up to?"

The boy looked at Timmy in amazement, marvelling

at his cycling helmet and shorts. He then looked more closely at Thandie, who tried to look as friendly as possible back.

The boy smiled a shy smile.

"Hello, my name is Mungwe. I am a Masai. My home is down in the south of Kenya, near the border with Tanzania. A few days ago, I got a lift to the market to sell my family's chickens, but the truck went to a market far, far away. I think my home is still many days walk from here. I have never been this far from home before."

"I know how that feels," replied Timmy. "We are really far from home too, but I am looking for my new home with my Uncle Max. I am going to help him with the elephants. Why don't we travel together for a bit. We can get you to your home much quicker and it will be nice for Thandie and me to have company."

Mungwe's smile became bigger and he quickly answered, "Oh yes, please! It is always nice to have company. Maybe the people in my village know where your Uncle Max lives and we can help you get there. It is very good that you want to help the elephants."

"Great, jump on. Let's go!"

Timmy, Thandie and Mungwe set off, heading south in the hot sun. After a couple of miles, there was an ear-splitting screech from Thandie's brakes and they all ended up in a heap on the side of the road.

Mungwe's Masai cloak had got caught up in the brakes. Luckily, they had not been going fast and no one was hurt. They got their breath back, looked at each other and started to laugh.

As they dusted themselves off and set off again, Timmy made a confession.

"Mungwe, we are a bit scared. We need to cycle through the game park. Will the lions chase us?"

Mungwe laughed. "Not the lions. They will be asleep now. They go hunting in the early morning and evening. Make sure you never cycle then. But we should look out for other animals. We should see a twiga, ngiri, swara, kiboko, tembo…"

Timmy looked confused. "What?"

Mungwe laughed again - "Those are the names in the Kenyan language. In English they are giraffe, warthog, impala, hippo, elephant…"

Timmy, Thandie and Mungwe saw all those animals that day.

"Don't go too close to the tembo," warned Mungwe, pointing to huge, grey shapes in the distance. "We wouldn't want them to charge at us; even on Thandie we would not stand a chance."

Hopefully I'll get to see lots of elephants when I get to Uncle Max's house, so no need to go close to them now, thought Timmy.

"Mind the tembo poo!" yelled Mungwe.

"That's the biggest poo I've ever seen!" laughed Timmy, as Thandie just managed to swerve around it.

Then the tallest animal they had ever seen strolled out from the trees. It must have been as tall as Mrs Haddock's house!

The giraffe stared at Thandie, and Thandie stared back. Then the giraffe started to run.

Thandie got faster

The giraffe got faster

Thandie got even faster

The giraffe got even faster

"He wants to race," shouted Mungwe.

Off they all went, faster and faster and faster...

"STOP!" screamed Mungwe.

Thandie screeched to a stop. With a shaking hand Mungwe pointed to a huge snake basking in the sun on the road.

"A puff adder," he whispered.

The puff adder looked

at them lazily out of one eye and as if trying to decide what to do next. Timmy went pale beneath his suntan and felt his heart beating faster and faster. Two boys from his school, James and Ben, who knew a lot about wildlife, had told him all about puff adders and he remembered them saying that they are the most poisonous snakes in the world. They all stared at the snake, not daring to move a muscle. Then, very, very slowly, the puff adder slithered off the road and disappeared into the bushes.

They looked around. The giraffe had disappeared.

Timmy, Mungwe and Thandie breathed a massive sigh of relief, smiled at each other weakly and set off again.

"My village is just a few miles further on," said Mungwe. "Thank you very much for the lift." He looked up at the sun. "But it will be dark soon. You must stay with me. You can meet all my family and we can plan the best way for you to find your Uncle Max."

Mungwe's village

"Wake up, lazybones!" he heard as Mungwe bounced into the room followed by about ten other children. "Everyone wants to meet you." Timmy followed Mungwe and the other children out of the hut. "First job is to go get some water. Can you and Thandie help? It will be much quicker and easier with Thandie."

"Of course," replied Timmy.

Mungwe attached two huge, plastic containers where the back panniers usually went. Timmy realised that some of the other children were getting on bikes with huge containers too. It was a very strange collection of bikes. Other than Thandie, most of the bikes were really old and although most were not as big as Thandie most were adult bikes, far too big for Mungwe's friends. But they were brilliant riders, able to ride standing up or crouching down. Some bikes had two or even three children on them, with one balancing on the handlebars and one on the saddle, whilst a third pedalled. The best cyclists were two girls called Esmae and Aggie who managed to keep their bike moving along whilst they kept changing places with each other as one pedalled and one ran alongside. Timmy was amazed at all the different bikes and at how skilful all the riders were. He stared at them all but then starting laughing when he realised that they were all staring back at him. They were just as amazed at the incredible Thandie!

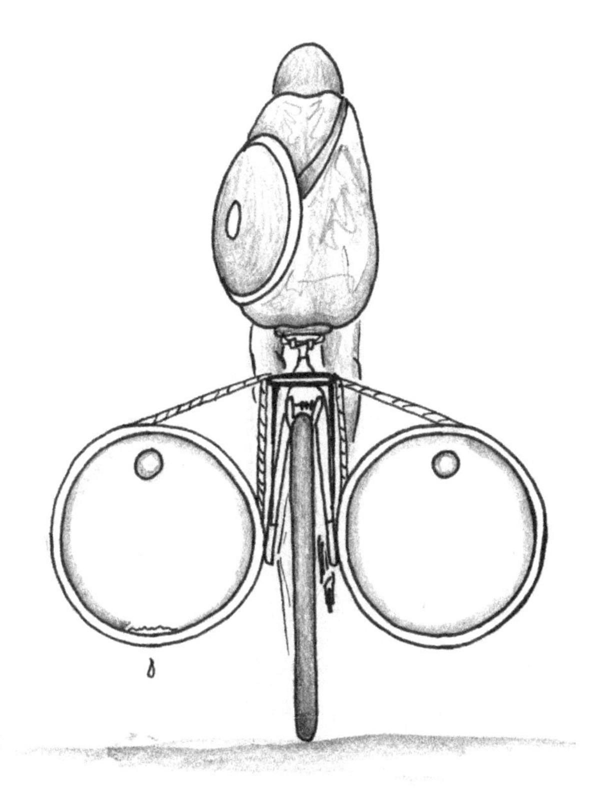

All the children and all the bicycles went off down the road. The noise was incredible – squeaking brakes, rubbing tyres, the padding of running feet and, most of all, the chattering of all the children, who had a million questions for Timmy, just as he had a million questions for them. The funny thing was, even though many of the answers were different (Mrs Haddock's house was very different from Mungwe's house and Timmy never saw elephants or giraffes in London), Timmy soon realised that there were more similarities than differences. He and Mungwe both liked football (although it was a shame Mungwe supported Man U, when Timmy supported Arsenal). They both hated Maths and loved History. They both had to do boring chores at home when all they really wanted to do was to run around outside with their friends.

After about twenty minutes they arrived at a water pump and then the serious business began – filling up all the containers. They were so heavy that Timmy was worried about whether Thandie would be able to manage them. Luckily Thandie was really strong. The journey home was much slower, though. Timmy thought he could hear Thandie puffing and panting under the weight of the water.

"Do you have to do this every day?" asked Timmy.

"Of course," replied Mungwe. "But it is quite fun when we all go together. Today, we are lucky, there is no school, so we can play games when we get home."

When they got back to the village they gave the water to the adults, who were very pleased with the amount of water Thandie had brought back.

"Let's play poachers and rangers," shouted Aggie.

"What's that?" asked Timmy.

"Poachers are the baddies, they kill the wild animals. They kill elephants for their tusks and rhinos for their horns. The rangers are the goodies and try to stop them," explained Esmae.

How horrible, thought Timmy. *I still cannot believe people want to kill elephants and rhinos. Uncle Max must be a ranger and Mr Kubwa must be a poacher.*

They all ran off into the bush, pretending to be hunting elephants or tracking poachers.

Timmy and Mungwe had a wonderful time together and Thandie had a very well-deserved rest but soon Timmy knew he had to leave. The game had made him remember why he and Thandie were travelling through Africa – to help Uncle Max save the elephants from the terrible poacher, Mr Kubwa.

Mr Kubwa

"My cousin, Felix, knows where your Uncle Max lives. If you and Thandie can take him home to the next village, he will show you the way."

"Brilliant. Thank you for letting me stay, please come to visit me at Uncle Max's house," said Timmy, saying goodbye to Mungwe. Then he asked eagerly, "Felix, can you tell me about where Uncle Max lives? Do you know my Uncle Max?"

Felix started talking as they pedalled down the road. "I have never been to his house but I know that he is a good man. He works very hard to protect our elephants. There are some bad people around here who try to take the elephants' tusks because the ivory is so valuable. The bad men, or poachers, will track elephants for miles with guns and then they will shoot them. When an elephant is dead they will hack off its tusks."

"Why do they need to kill the elephants?" asked Timmy.

"How else will they get the tusks?" Felix replied. "Do you think an elephant will just stand still and let someone cut off its tusks? Would you stand still and let someone cut off your ears? The poachers do not care about the animals and so the easiest thing is to kill them."

"But why?' asked Timmy, feeling very upset and angry.

"Ivory is very valuable in a lot of countries, and there are some nasty businessmen who know that they can make a lot of money. It is a hard life for many men here and they can earn more as a poacher than anything else. I know some men who don't want to be poachers, but they need the money for their families. But that is the problem. Once you are in a poacher's gang it is very hard to leave. You would know all their secrets and they would not want you reporting them to the rangers."

Timmy understood what Felix was saying about the poachers needing to make money but he still could not understand how someone could kill an elephant just to sell its tusks.

"So, what does my Uncle Max do?" asked Timmy, eager to hear more about his only relative.

"Max is very famous around here. He tries to find jobs for the poor men so that that they do not need to become poachers. He makes sure that there are lots of rangers and that they are all trained properly. He is also trying to make sure everyone knows that poaching is bad. Did you know that some people think that having ivory is OK? They think that if you cut off a tusk, a new one will grow back and they don't realise that the elephants are killed. Max's main enemy is Mr Kubwa. This means 'big' in Swahili. He is head of the biggest and meanest poaching gang. You do not want to get mixed up with him…"

Wow, thought Timmy. *Uncle Max has a lot of jobs to do. I hope I can help him.*

Timmy, Thandie and Felix pedalled on a bit more in silence. Timmy's mind was spinning with thoughts of elephants, poachers, the terrible Mr Kubwa and his Uncle Max.

Felix broke into Timmy's thoughts.

"My village is just up here, thank you for the lift. You will find your Uncle Max about a day's ride more, just follow this road. But beware of the poachers. There will be lots of them around as we have seen many elephants recently and there is one enormous bull elephant with huge tusks nearby. I am sure Mr Kubwa's gang will be after him."

"Bye Felix. Don't worry, I'll be careful," shouted Timmy, waving as he and Thandie pedalled onwards.

A few miles later Timmy saw some large, dark-coloured birds circling overhead.

They must be vultures, he thought. *They fly over dying animals, waiting to eat the dead bodies. I wonder what it is? Maybe it is not dead yet, maybe I can help.*

He steered off the road heading towards the vultures. Thandie tried hard to stop him, she pulled back, but Timmy just pedalled harder so she had to give in to him. They bumped across the rough scrubland for a bit, trying to avoid the big holes and thorny bushes. Finally, they came across a terrible sight. They saw a huge elephant lying on the ground with blood seeping into the grass and sand. Timmy knew at once that the elephant was dead and that there was nothing he could do. Yet he was rooted to the spot. He just stared and stared at the great animal not realising that tears were streaming down his cheeks.

Suddenly he heard a noise behind him. He turned and stared up, high up into the eyes of the biggest man he had ever seen. He was as tall as a house and his arms were as big as tree trunks. He had a big scar on his cheek and terrifying tattoos on his neck and chest. He was holding a gun. Behind this giant were more men, all enormous, all with guns.

'Mr Kubwa,' he whispered and he opened his mouth to scream.

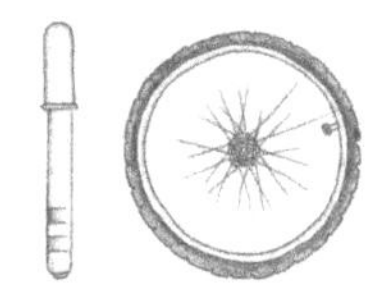

Timmy and Thandie go poaching

"Quiet," came a growl and a hand as big as a dinner plate was put over Timmy's mouth. The big man with the gun continued, "As soon as it starts to get dark, you and your bike are going to take me into the bush to find that bull elephant. He has the best tusks I have ever seen and WE are going to get them."

"How will you get them?" whispered Timmy, scared that he already knew the answer.

"With my little friend here," said the man, pointing at his gun, with a horrible smile.

Timmy felt sick. He looked at Thandie and was sure that Thandie was looking sad and her handlebars seemed to be shaking.

"Sorry, Thandie, but I don't see what else we can do." Thandie looked even more upset.

Mr Kubwa turned to the other men. "Right. A new plan. I am going to go on this strange bike with this silly little boy to find that elephant. You all follow on foot as back-up. Remember your guns."

"What will we do with him?" asked one of the men, pointing at Timmy.

"We'll see how useful he is and then decide," said Mr Kubwa with a nasty look in his eyes.

Timmy cowered closer to Thandie. In a voice far braver than he felt he asked, "But what about the rangers? I have heard that they are nearby and they have guns too. They will catch you."

"They might," said the big man, "but they won't be expecting a poacher on a bike. If they catch me they catch you, too, and they won't like little boys who help poachers."

Timmy felt even more sick but he knew the poacher was right. If they were caught by the rangers, then the elephant would be safe but he and Thandie might not be. Not unless he could persuade the rangers he was not part of the poaching gang. Maybe the rangers would know Uncle Max, but they might not believe Timmy, and Uncle Max might not even recognise him.

Mr Kubwa continued addressing his men.

"The elephant was probably heading towards the watering hole to the west. We have seen a family there too, so even if we don't get the big bull we might still find some good ivory. But the aim is to get the bull. His tusks would mean we could retire!" He laughed and turned to Timmy. "Right. No noise, no lights. Do exactly what I say, or else… Let's go!"

Timmy and Mr Kubwa got onto Thandie and started pedalling. Thandie tried as hard as she could not to move.

"Pedal faster," grunted the poacher.

"Come on, Thandie, we need to go," whispered Timmy.

Then they were off, bumping across the rough grass. They went past lots of chattering monkeys who looked at them in surprise. They went past a family of zebra, who swished their tails in greeting. They went past two tall giraffes, chewing on leaves from the tops of the trees. For the first time Timmy did not enjoy looking at these animals.

"Stop!" growled Mr Kubwa in a very loud whisper. "The watering hole is just up here." Timmy, Thandie and Mr Kubwa slowly made their way forwards. "There!" the poacher whispered.

Timmy looked up and saw the biggest elephant he had ever seen. It was as big as a red London bus and its tusks seemed almost to touch the ground. The elephant was scratching himself against a tree.

Then, suddenly, all at once, several terrifying things happened.

The huge elephant turned at looked directly at them.

"He must have smelt us," whispered the poacher. "Stay very still."

Timmy and Thandie froze.

The elephant made the loudest trumpeting sound Timmy had ever heard, flapped its ears and prepared to charge at them.

The poacher levelled his gun at the huge animal.

Timmy shut his eyes. A shot rang out. Either the elephant was going to trample them or the poacher had killed it.

But then the poacher yelled and fell to the side. His weight made Thandie and Timmy fall over. They all ended up in a dusty heap on the ground.

"My leg," sobbed the poacher. Timmy realised the poacher had blood seeping through his trousers.

Timmy did not understand until he saw a shadow and heard another voice.

"Well, well, well! Finally, we have got you, Mr Kubwa. We found the rest of your gang earlier and now we have the big boss." He then looked at Timmy. "We seem to have found a young poacher too. Good, we have caught you before you can hurt any animals."

"What happened?" whispered Timmy.

"Luckily for you, the elephant changed his mind when he heard my shot and went in the other direction. Elephants are very clever animals. Much cleverer than poachers. You are both coming with me. You are both under arrest."

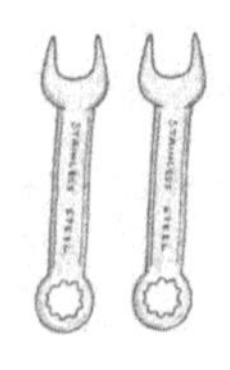

Uncle Max

The head ranger gestured to his men and Timmy and Mr Kubwa were roughly pushed onto a truck.

"What about Thandie?" asked Timmy pointing at his bicycle, still lying forlornly in the dust.

With grunts and groans, the rangers lifted Thandie up and tied her to the top of the truck.

"Be careful with her," pleaded Timmy.

"You have more important things to worry about, boy," snarled the angry ranger. Then the truck set off, bumping across the rough ground.

Mr Kubwa was still bleeding from his gun-shot wound and he moaned with every bump, but he kept looking at Timmy with evil eyes.

"You need to be careful, don't tell them anything."

Timmy sat in silence, trying very hard not to cry. He could not decide whether he was more scared of the ranger or of Mr Kubwa and he was really worried about Thandie.

Then they stopped. Timmy heard the front door of the truck slam shut and then he heard low voices.

These must be rangers and they must know Uncle Max, Timmy thought to himself.

He shouted out, "Please, do you know my Uncle…" but Timmy didn't get to finish his sentence. Mr Kubwa silenced him with a rough push and a glare. He remembered Mr Kubwa's threats and the warnings from Felix. He stopped talking and sat, trembling, in the truck.

The ranger roughly pulled him out and pushed him down onto the ground. Thandie was already off the truck, propped up against a tree. His dark brown eyes glared at Timmy. He was a very big man too, although not as big as Mr Kubwa. He looked very strong and powerful but he did not look as terrifying as Timmy had first thought.

"Please. I am not a poacher," Timmy began.

The ranger gave a half smile. "I didn't really think you were," he said. "But I am not sure what to do with you. You did help by guiding us with your light. If we hadn't seen your light then Mr Kubwa could have shot the elephant."

"The light?" asked Timmy in surprise. Then he looked across at Thandie. Her back light flashed on and off quickly. "Of course," said Timmy quickly. "We knew you must be nearby, so we turned on the light so you could follow us. Do you work with my Uncle Max? He sent for me."

The ranger's eyes widened in surprise. "Of course I know Max. He did mention his nephew was coming to help. But, how do I know you are who you say you are? Wait there." He walked off a little way and took his radio from his pocket and barked some instructions.

Timmy huddled closer to Thandie, knowing that the next few minutes could decide whether he found his uncle or whether he went to prison with Mr Kubwa and his gang.

An older man, but still very big and strong, came running over. He looked even more angry than the rangers and Mr Kubwa, Timmy shrank back and tried to hide. Then this man gave a start and made a low whistling sound as he spotted them by the tree. "Well I never, Thandie!" he peered behind Thandie, "Timmy?" he asked.

"Yes" came a whisper. "Are you my Uncle Max?" Timmy slowly got to his feet and looked up into the piercing blue eyes staring down at him.

Max ruffled Timmy's hair, messing it up even more than normal. "I would recognize you anywhere, you look just like your father did when he was your age. You've certainly got the family hair." Timmy doubtfully looked up at the shiny, bald head. "You probably don't believe me but I used to have hair just like yours!" Uncle Max explained with a small smile. Then his smile disappeared and he looked sternly at Timmy. "I knew I could count on Thandie to bring you to me. But I didn't think you would arrive like this. Why are you mixed up with Mr Kubwa? I am very upset that you have both been helping the poachers." He looked again at Thandie, "Thandie, you should know better, I am very ashamed of you too."

Thandie looked very sad.

However, despite looking very angry, it did look as if there was a spark of kindness in Uncle Max's eyes. Timmy felt braver than he had in a long time.

"I am not a poacher," he began in a rush. "I hate the poachers. Thandie and I did not want to help them. Thandie tried really hard not to let us but I made her. Mr Kubwa made us. He threatened us with his gun. We didn't have a choice. She turned on the back light so the rangers could follow us."

Max looked at the ranger. He nodded.

"Well, Mr Kubwa is a very evil man and it sounds as though you and Thandie did everything you could," Uncle Max went on. "Luckily, no elephants were hurt today and, even better, we have captured Mr Kubwa and his whole gang. That means the elephants will be safe around here for a bit longer."

"Does that mean you are out of a job?" asked Timmy.

"Oh no, just because we have this gang, it does not mean that the elephants are safe. There are other gangs who try to poach elephants and there are other animals in danger too, like rhinos. There's still lots of work to be done."

"Then you still want me to stay and help you?" asked Timmy hopefully.

"Of course I do!" replied Uncle Max with a big grin.

Timmy looked back at Mr Kubwa, who was still glaring at him.

"But what's going to happen to the poachers?"

"Don't worry about them. They are off to prison for a very long time," replied Max. "Now, let's go home and you can tell me all about your adventures."

Timmy thought back to the start of his journey, to leaving London, Mrs Haddock and George. He thought about Florence, his first new friend. He thought about following the Nile, about Nefertiti and the curse of the pharaohs. He thought about nearly running out of water in the desert. He thought about Mungwe and Felix. He thought about the elephants and all the amazing animals. Finally, he thought about his best friend, Thandie.

"Oh yes, we have some adventures to tell you, Uncle Max."

Note from the author

In real life Thandie is ridden by Stuart. On their adventures Mungwe, a Masai, really did get his cloak stuck in the brakes; they really did ride through the desert; a giraffe really did race them; they met lots of rangers (but luckily no poachers) and they saw lots of amazing animals. Stuart was joined on many of his adventures by his wife, Claire, who has written this story. Stuart and Claire are both teachers and have joined forces with illustrator Tim, another teacher and tandem cyclist, for this book. Find out more about Stuart, Claire and Thandie's adventures at www.beyondthebike.org

There is a real Max (who still has lots of hair!), the founder of Space for Giants. This charity protects Africa's elephants from immediate threats like poaching while working to secure their habitats in landscapes facing greatly-increasing pressures. Stuart and Thandie have supported Space for Giants since staying with Max in Kenya in 2012. For more information go to www.spaceforgiants.org.

Beyond the Bike has raised nearly £200,000 for various charities since 2011. Half of any profits from this book will go to Space for Giants and Beyond Ourselves (an Educational Charity based in Zambia supported by Beyond the Bike since 2011).

There are many more stories to tell and so look out for more Thandie the Tandem books coming soon.